THE COWBOY'S CHRISTMAS

THE COWBOY'S CHRISTMAS

JOAN WALSH ANGLUND

A Margaret K. McElderry Book

ATHENEUM 1972 NEW YORK

TO THE COWBOY'S TEACHERS

Miss Vail

Mrs. Fulton

Miss Hilton

Mr. Birnbaum

Mr. Steinert

Mrs. Grenfell

Copyright © 1972 by Joan Walsh Anglund
All rights reserved
Library of Congress catalog card number 70-190551
Published simultaneously in Canada by McClelland & Stewart, Ltd.
Manufactured in the United States of America
Printed by Connecticut Printers, Inc., Hartford
Bound by A. Horowitz & Son/Bookbinders, Clifton, New Jersey
First Printing May 1972
Second Printing June 1972

724959

Once there was a cowboy . . .

who was Especially Busy,

(and so was his friend, Bear).

Every day he had a lot to do.
Some days he wrote things . . .

and some days he made things . . .

. . . and some days

and some days he made things . . .

. . . and some days

he just wished for things.

But *every* day . . . he was Busy!

But no matter how Busy he was,

the cowboy was never cross . . .
he was never fretful.

Somehow, the cowboy
was Especially Polite.

Somehow, the cowboy
never seemed
to cause trouble any more.

Somehow, the cowboy always seemed
to be helpful lately,

(and so was Bear).

Somehow, the cowboy
was Especially Good.

Now, each day seemed busier
than the day before.

The cowboy went shopping . . .

the cowboy baked cookies . . .

the cowboy wrapped boxes . . .

the cowboy ran errands,
        (and Bear always helped) .

He took things down . . .

he put things up.

But no matter
where he went . . .

no matter how much he had to do . . .

somehow . . . the cowboy was Especially Cheerful.

Then, one snowy night,

the cowboy
hung up his stocking . . .

DECEMBER
24

said his prayers,
and went to sleep . . .

to dream a Very Special Dream.

And the next morning,

the cowboy had a Very Merry Christmas.

He hopes *you* will have one too!